A Prepared People

By Iamgood Chinenye Momah-Eze Barr.Evg

A Prepared People

ISBN: 978-978-57859-1-3

Amazon with Kindle Direct Publishing

Email: iamgoodchinenye@gmail.com

Let him kiss me with the kisses of his mouth:

for thy love is   better than wine.

I am Black but comely, O ye daughters of Jerusalem,

as the tents of ke-dar, as the

Curtains of Solomon.

Look not upon me, because I am black, because

the sun hath looked upon me: my

Mother's children were angry with me; they

made me the keeper of the vineyards;

But mine own vineyard have I not kept.

I am the rose of Sharon, and the lily of the val-

leys.

As the lily among thorns, so is my

love among the daughters.

He brought me to the banqueting house

and his banner over me was love.

Songs of Solomon: verses from chapter 1 and 2 KJV

Preface

This is a book designated to prepare the people for the kingdom of GOD. It is designed to make the believer emerge as a born again and to be heavenly conscious in order not to be taken unawares at the coming of Jesus Christ. It will aid in living a victorious Christian life and that it is possible that GODs kingdom can come on earth if we only believe. A Prepared People is an eye opener, See the kingdom of GOD is at hand!

Table of contents

Chapter 1: Salvation is of the Jews.

Guess what! No other religion, but Christianity is the true religion and it all originated from the Jews.

To be GODs prepared people you have to realise that Salvation is of the Jews, that your salvation lies in Jesus Christ alone.

Christianity all started from the sect of the Jews whom have walked with Jesus, called as his disciples and who were given that special mandate by our Lord Jesus Christ in Matthew 28:19-20

Go ye therefore and teach all nations baptizing them in the name of the father and of the son and of the Holy Ghost:

Teaching them to observe all things whatsoever I have commanded you and lo I am with you always, even unto the end of the world. Amen.

We didn't learn of Christianity without being spoken to, not that we can't be spoken to directly by the holy ghost to repent as was the case of Cornelius who was ministered to by an angel directly from GOD and told to send for peter but yet an apostle was sent for by Cornelius even after seeing an angel of GOD hence salvation has come to us mostly by the work of the Apostles, Disciples who obeyed the instruction of Jesus and went about the preaching of the gospel. Wow!

I tell you, Jesus was at a well one particular day and got into dialogue with a certain Samaritan woman; asking her to give him water to drink and the woman's reply was *how can you a Jew ask of me water, which am a woman of Samaria for the Jews have no dealings with the Samaritans.*

After conversation about the living water, thereon he asked her to call her husband. The woman replied, *Sir I perceive that thou art a prophet. She saying our fathers worshipped in this mountain and ye say that in Jerusalem is the place where men ought to worship.* Jesus said unto her, Woman believe me, the hour cometh when ye shall neither in this mountain, nor in Jerusalem worship the Father. Ye worship ye know not what: we know what we worship: for salvation is of the Jews.

But the hour cometh and now is, when the true wor-shippers shall worship the father in spirit and in truth: for the father seeketh such to worship him. GOD is a spirit: and they that worship him must worship in spirit and in truth.

The Abraham covenant is contained in Genesis 17 and Genesis 22 vs. 16-18.

Genesis 22 Vs 16-18: And said, By myself have I sworn saith the Lord, for because thou has done this thing and has not withheld thine son, thine only son: that in blessing I will bless thee and in multiplying I will multiply thy seed as the stars of heaven, and as the sand which is upon the sea shore; and thy seed shall possess the gate of his enemies.

The son of GOD came from King David's lineage, the son of Abraham. GOD is wonderful, all we have learnt, have been learnt by Jews. The Israelites Ist received the lord Jesus Christ and the 12 apostles –the apostles minus 1 who was to be replaced as recorded in acts 1 vs. 23-26 with Mathias first received the Holy Ghost.

The prophets of old made mention of the lord Jesus Christ, one of which is Isaiah who declares in chapter 9 vs. 6-8:

For unto us a child is born, unto us a son is given: and the government shall be upon his shoulder: and his name shall be called Wonderful, Counsellor, The mighty God, The everlasting Father, The Prince of Peace. Of the increase of his government and peace there shall be no end, upon the throne of David and upon his kingdom, to order it, and from henceforth even forever. The zeal of the Lord of hosts will perform this. The Lord sent a word unto Jacob and it hath lighted upon Israel.

There's no way to GOD the Father, unless through the son.

The Prepared people are those who have washed their garment clean I need to say this over again. When one wants to do a wedding he readily prepares. Jesus said 'no one can come to the son except the father draws him' he likewise says, No one knows the Father but the Son and the son but the father and whosoever he 'the Son' reveals the father to.

Acts 1 records that Jesus told the Apostles to wait for the promise of the father – the Holy Ghost.

There's nothing GOD will not speak to you of that will not be still redirected to the scriptures. He said "they shall all be taught of GOD" that we will need no man or anyone to teach us.

Do we really appreciate that "Salvation is of the Jews" Are we finding it difficult to keep GODs

Words, the instructions of the Holy Ghost by the apostles. Really what is going on with your Christianity? Romans 5:17 says

But GOD be thanked that ye were the servants of sin, but ye have obeyed from the heart that form of doctrine which was delivered to you.

There's a doctrine that was delivered to the Gentiles by the Apostles. An instruction unto holiness, righteousness, salvation by Grace.

There are people who hazarded their lives for the sake of Christ, people who shed their blood, who lived in deplorable conditions, who endured hardship for the sake of you and me. Now would you choose the word of GOD to keep and the one to do away with? Jesus says in a verse in revelation repent from whence ye have fallen.

Heaven and earth will pass away, but his word will never pass away. To be saved by grace is a beautiful thing.

Heb 11:1-40 recounts those who have walked with GOD through faith and have triumphed. Verse 6 of that 11 say's:

But without faith it is impossible to please him for he that cometh to GOD must believe he is and that he is a rewarder of them that diligently seek him.

See Hebrews 10:16, Romans 11.

Remember, *who are Israelites; to whom pertaineth the adoption, and the glory and the covenants and the giving of the law, and the service of GOD and the promises; whose are the fathers, and of whom as concerning the flesh Christ came, who is over all GOD blessed forever. Amen.*

Not as though the word of GOD hath taken none effect. For they are not all Israel, which are of Israel:

Neither, because they are the seed of Abraham, are they all children: but, in Isaac shall thy seed be called.

That is they which are the children of the flesh; these are not the children of GOD: but the children of the promise are counted for the seed.

There's no way into GODs Kingdom, without coming through the son – "Our lord Jesus Christ"

His name be praised!

Chapter 2: Consensus & Meeting of the Apostles

Wow! What took place on that glorious day? Well I would just have you know that consensus means meeting of the minds. It culminates to an agreement. On that glorious day the apostles met to decide one very **trivial** issue how you and me ("not that we are still gentiles since we are Israelites by faith") can be saved. It's written in the book of Acts 15.

And it states that certain Pharisees who believed came up with the idea that the gentiles should keep the Law of Moses. Then the apostles and the elders considered the matter and agreed within themselves as vs. 28-29 states

For it seemed good to the Holy Ghost, and to us to lay upon you no greater burden than these necessary things:

"That ye abstain from meats offered to idols and from blood, and from things strangled, and from fornication: from which if ye keep yourselves, ye shall do well. Fare ye well".

The bible says can 2 walk together unless they agree. Where the spirit of GOD is there is liberty. When two or 3 come together and agree touching anything on earth, it is done for them by the father in heaven.

This agreement was sent to brethren who are

of gentiles at Antioch, Syria and Cilicia. Today Antioch is present day Turkish Antakya, Syria is present day Syrian Arab Republic and Cilicia is present day Southern Mediterranean coast of Turkey.

Every decision made is made with Jesus knowing full well that the Holy Ghost is that comforter, the spirit of truth whom Jesus promised to send to the disciples in fact they were told to wait for him and anything he says he has heard from Jesus. As the scriptures says. Moreover in the book of revelation 2:20, we were told that Jesus was displeased with the church saying:

Notwitstanding I have a few things against thee, because thou sufferest that woman Jezebel, which calleth herself a prophetess, to teach and to seduce my servants to commit fornication,and to eat things

sacrificed unto idols.

vs 21: *"And I gave her space to repent of her fornica-*

tion; and she repented not"

The essence of the conclusion in Acts 15 is found in that Acts 15 from verse 19:-

Wherefore my sentence is that we trouble not them,

which from among the gentiles are turned to GOD.

Is GOD not so merciful how wonderful and merciful he is.

How easy salvation has come to the non- Jews and to think that we are counted as Israelites by faith and the original Jews are Israelites of promise.

We have come under this promise by faith.

Halleluyah! Amen!

Hence pertaining to the promise, you need no man to teach you. About the commandments Christ summed them up as two and presented it unto us, namely Love the Lord your GOD with all your soul, mind and body. Lastly Love thy neighbour as you love thyself. See Hebrews 10:16

Hallelujah! GOD's laws are in our hearts and minds. Praise GOD!

Natural instincts that we should honour our parents because we grew under them and were nurtured from child birth till we come of age.if you can greet elders along the way then you can greet your parents. We know that morality frowns at taking things not ours called stealing hence we should not covet our neighbours property notwithstanding what it is.

Honestly prepared people have repented of their past life of sin. We must no longer engage in vices or whatever ills or illicit acts. **Fornication should not be named amongst us because the will of GOD is our sanctification that we even abstain from fornication.**

We can do away with whatever GODS prepared people should not handle; those lies on tv, those unwholesome gossip in newspapers, magazines, Those medias selling fornication and be occupied with Jesus be submerged whole in the Holy Ghost. Be filled with the spirit.

I am sure the Holy Ghost will pin point our grey areas to us and work on us. Its written be ye perfect as your GOD is perfect. Amen!

Heaven is a place for Prepared People. Do you wish to be amongst them.

Then take a stand, take that bold step, you can't be left behind in life. That glorious abode is for you and me.

Rules on marriages should not be done away with. Remember Jesus says that they which shall be accounted worthy to obtain that world and the resurrection from the dead neither marry nor are given in marriage neither can they die anymore. For they are equal unto the angels and are children of GOD, being the children of the resurrection. As believers we should adhere to the instructions of the apostles about marriage leading a quiet life in subjection to GOD. Scriptures on marriage are contained in 1st Corinthians 7, 1 Timothy 2:1-5 and 3:1-16, 1 Peter 3:1-8, Matthew 19:1-12, Mark 10:1-12, Luke 20:35. The rest may be found in the old testament which we can check online by our self at our quiet times or recreational time.

I don't think theres anymore for us to here than this lets not be unbelieving

Lest a promise of entering into GODs rest is denied us.

We can, We are GODs people, and We can be GODs Prepared people.

We are GODs prepared people. Amen!

Halleluyah!

Chapter 3: Doctrine (A talk on Women, Marriage, the church)

Being a woman, one thing we should know that GOD has fully equipped women on the earth for so much. Remember the creation of eve the purpose was for man not to be alone and the responsibility to be fruitful and to till the earth.

There's so much that women are used for in this earth and we women can be so productive to help GOD bring about his expected end for us.

There are so many women in the bible that GOD used to do great things like Sarah, who brought forth Isaac, Rebekah who brought forth Jacob,

Hannah who had Samuel, Deborah the Prophetess, Manaoah and his wife who had Samson, Elizabeth who had John the Baptist, Mary who gave us our Lord Jesus Christ.

Women are used for procreation and are useful hand maids in GOD hands; why not let that light in you be used to give glory to GOD.

One thing GOD has made me know when it comes to the issue of modesty is that it still points back to our culture. You find yourself being modest and still preserving your culture or tradition and the way things should ordinarily be. When I chose to really try hard to keep the biblical standards of Modesty it preserved me as a Nigerian Woman. The true Identity of my creation and race was preserved. Here I don't mean the ancient dress code of Natives of Nigeria which were often revealing but I mean the true Identity that GOD desires or desired for an African Nigerian Woman.

I would honestly tell you that the reason to not adorn or dress in a certain way as a woman is not because its evil or has an evil attached to it but because it's an instruction and you don't do it because those that gave that instruction received it from the holy ghost and meant well for us. It's not to look down on you or to make you look less beautiful but that holy women of old did no such thing.

I would just take this all over again and be explicit. On the Modesty of a woman I say, the word of GOD says extremely modest. Yes there are trousers that are modest; but do they pass the test of extremely modest, let's forget the old testament doctrine of not wearing what pertains to a man because we don't keep all the laws, if we choose to remember it, it's because its accompanied by abomination to GOD. We know that the book of revelation says that the abominable shall not be allowed to enter GODs kingdom. Men, women, for the fear of GOD, love and Awe please be on the save side. Do away with all appearance of unrighteousness. I know we are not to judge a person by his outward appearance but a tree is known by its fruit and we can't take new wine and put in old wine skin or bottle lets be true children of our father in heaven even in the entirety.

About Jewelries,Jeremiah says a bride does not forget her ornaments or a maid her jewellery but you have forgotten me the fountain of life.

So like Paul the Apostle, like peter, not with Gold jewellery, pearls. Let it not be that outward adorning of plaiting the hair and of wearing of gold or putting on of apparel. Why use gold or pearls jewelleries there are other jewelleries why use jewellery at all. You may say Sarah wore Jewelleries and Rebekah received a box of Jewellries as gifts, remember then there was no Law and Prophet, there was no Jesus Christ teachings or Apostles teachings by Holy Ghost. Please it is solely an instruction given by forerunners in faith of us. I know we are no longer under the Law.

Why wear bedes they even mean prayers you may just be wearing a bede prayed on, for a purpose you may not be in support of. Jacobs's house removed all the strange GODs and earrings from their ears and he covenanted his house with GOD. Do you not want to be a part of that covenant house. You may find out that doing away with that ring on your ear means coming under that covenant, Jacobs lineage down to king david and joseph brought forth Christ. Yes Christ is a better covenant and to the pure all things are pure and what about the instructions of GOD through Christ, through his apostles. Please women we are fearfully and wonderfully made. Not speaking heresies or being a fanatic, this way you pray is it the way

GOD has thought us to pray. You love the agnostics, I too love them and all they suffered for Christ how they learnt to pray but Jesus said when you pray, pray this way Our father who art in heaven... why disobey. Remember there's no enchantment against Israel or divination against Jacob stick to instructions and have a glorious Christian life and you can never be denied entrance into GODs kingdom. Remember *Exodus 20:4 "thou shalt not make unto thee any graven image or any likeness of anything that is in heaven above, or that is in the earth beneath, or that is in the water under the earth.*

Remember Galatians 1:6-9

'I marvel that ye are so soon removed from him that called you into the grace of Christ unto another gos-

pel: which is not another; but there be some that trouble you and would pervert the gospel of Christ.

But though we, or an angel from heaven, preach any other gospel unto you than that which we have preached unto you, let him be accursed.

For do I now persuade men or God? Or do I seek to please men? For if I yet pleased men, I should not be the servant of Christ

But I certify you brethren that the gospel which was preached of me is not after man.

Vs 12: For I neither received it of man neither was I taught it, but by the revelation of Jesus Christ.

Please I would repeat and say; where have you gotten your gospel from. What have you been thought about making it into GODs kingdom? Where did you get your gospel of salvation? We must go for the word. The word of GOD is tested, tried and true. There is a form of doctrine that was delivered unto us. *Romans 6:17:*

"But GOD be thanked, that ye were the servants of sin but ye have obeyed from the heart that form of doctrine, which was delivered to you.

On African women do you know what GOD revealed to me, on modesty, it is made known to me that it dates back to our nativity or culture where we are from. I realised that when I started keeping the doctrine of apostle paul and peter on modesty I was conforming to the image of being African an African Nigerian woman. I began to see myself as Igbo, even though an Israelite by faith. These rules are not stringent. A reprobate mind does not retain GOD and cant understand the things of GOD says the book of romans.

Please Nigerians we don't need the relaxing of our hair, women stop the painting of your face which we hide and say it's make up. Let me chip in something remember Jezebel that Phoenician princess who was a wife to Ahab I read she painted her eye when Jehu... came and looked thru the window. I didnt really like preachers using her as an example to say women should not use makeup for the reason that she used makeup, I felt its wrong to say women should not use make up that Jezebel used it that its a sin but I have a deeper understanding now that this practice is associated with pagans those who are non Jews. You won't have a real Israeli or Jew

on makeup. I don't think they enlarge their eyes

so then we can do away with all appearance of

unrighteousness. You may want to use Esther to

say she adorned but remember Esther was in a

strange land she solely adorned for the purpose

of the king to get her into that marriage. The use

of makeup is certainly not a custom associated

with GOD it came forth from pagan practice or

from them that are non Jews.

We are truly fearfully and wonderfully made.

We are Israelites by Faith. GOD help us, GOD

bless Nigeria.

 Halleluyah!

Every word of GOD is breathed by the

Holy Ghost profitable for reproof, for direc-

tion in holiness that the workman may be fully

equipped...have no need to be ashamed rightly

dividing the word of truth.

Chapter 4: Resign to faith not your faith

Peter denied Jesus 3 times

Yet he led the life his master desired of him

His weaknesses did not take the better part of him.

Beloved now we are the sons of GOD; and it doth not yet appear what we shall be; but we know that when he shall appear we shall be like him for we shall see him as he is.

For the prophecy came not in old time by the will

of man: but holy men of GOD spake as they were

moved by the Holy Ghost.

All scripture is given by the inspiration of GOD and

is profitable for doctrine for reroof for correction

for instruction in righteousness. That the man of

GOD may be perfect thoroughly furnished unto all

good works.

Ist John 3:2, 2nd peter 1:21, 2nd timothy 3:16-17

Faith is the assurance of things hope for the be-

lieve in things not yet seen, this is the **bedrock**

of Christianity. That should be the case of every

believer, even if your situation is so pathetic or

that you are designated for destruction resign

to faith that what the word of GOD says concerning your life will be and not those negative thoughts or confession that you have concluded pertaining to your life.

Faith says GODs words are yea and amen! Your faith can't see anything good coming, but you can marry that your faith with faith (GODs Word) and bring a glorious end. That is the way to work with GOD. The doctor just told you that you have an incurable disease and then you are not so strong in believe but you begin to think on what GOD has prepared for you,a glorious home coming and heaven a place where there is no sickness weeping and crying, you don't conform to the world but you are transformed by the renewing of your mind, your hope does not end in this world alone, so you can't see that situation, you gladly use your wheel chair while you get weaker because you are only see-ing yourself get closer to your final home,that is marrying that your faith with faith,you don't see anything with what people say only the son of GOD,you are over joyed, then you are sure in for a healing even an unexpected visitation by GOD for appreciating that his grace is sufficient unto you. Or you can not resign to that faith but faith by being assured that theres a great healer one who can cure your disease and so you begin to use GODs word against that infirmity, you call on the elders of your church to help you pray always concerning that situation, you put programs on healing for that very purpose because you resign to faith not your faith your faith says you are destroyed dead you are to be trampled upon dependent on people disregarded and maltreated, that you are pitiable but you insist on GODs word,that faith that we received on the day of redemption.

The situation with GODs people is that they are people who either marry. Their faith with Faith (as in the ist scenario given) or resign to faith not their faith. Every born again should let GODs faith be seen in his life, should not be ruled by the condition or situation he is in but be ruled by GODs word.

The prepared people of GOD have learnt to depend on GOD, they are sure unmoved by situation because they know that those who know their GOD shall be strong and do exploits. That is what GOD wants from us. He doesn't need you engaging in gossip over your spouse because his terrible in personality. He needs you inculcating the heavenly temperament which is the fruits of the spirit. To be among the prepared people is to allow GODs word rule you by being led by the spirit of GOD, remember the words Jesus spoke he said they are spirit and Life.

So then receive GODs word which is able to save your soul. I can't see any reason to be less of GODs faith but I can see every reason to be less of that your faith that does not correspond to the good thought GOD has for you.

    1. Its a lie from the enemy
    2. Its double mindedness

3. Its a deception
4. Its only interested in robbing you of life and a lasting relationship with GOD.

GOD prepares people when they go by his word, he would continually bring his word to his people for them to be helped. His a faithful friend and he has good intentions towards us all.

With my work with GOD I have had to re-sign to faith and not my faith, I realised that everything I have gone true and am going true was just to prepare me for the work ahead and to even prepare me for GODs kingdom. As at 2016 I was told by GOD that I would be a book writer, yet but with things that tran-spired I ignored and continued sitting at an office I even deviated and had less of it at heart but as at 2018 GOD still redirected me to this ministry and here I am able to articulate and construct **by GODs** spirit and to inform you of what GOD will have you know. Hence this book is by the spirit of GOD his the original author of the book, I am only an instrument or vessel used to bring about the expectation that he has before now established and designated to come.

So I am inculcating the heavenly principle that GOD will have me inform to those who are unaware or to bring to a reminder those who knew and may have forgotten. Resign to faith not your faith.

Chapter 5: Make a move

Sticks and stones do give GOD praise

And sticks are used to light a Fire

While stones are used to build a House

Even sticks may likewise do the same

Don't just sit there, do something about it?
You heard your wife just got pregnant, it made
you tipsy with joy, you both just (got married)
tied the knot and you only admired her just less
than 6 months she's with child, you recall her

coyness while at the university those days you used to see her talk quietly with a close friend of yours and every time she did see you she lightly wave her hands and put on a warm smile and it got you thinking how attractive this woman was, along the line you summoned up (on the) courage and approached her for something more and the remaining 2 years of your stay back at the university was a love to remember, you weren't the natural Christian folk or brother but now you got married you and Maria are not interested in giving any place to the devil, every day you want to adore those eyes of hers and the rest you adore to yourself, so you start doing something about it, it comes to you and her becoming fans of a particular marriage minister and then you both want to read the psalms of the bible together.

You don't just sit there this came on a Plata of gold, you start doing something about it. You cut off every wrong association, you cease to attend your football matches on days set apart for your fellowships, your bible comes in handy, you pray those words and every time you see that belly grow your prayer becomes more **intensified**.

You made that move early from love because you had good intentions with the lady Maria that you married and now you don't just sit there, you make a move.

The prepared people of GOD are those who may not have originally started with GOD but took the first step or made a move and became of the sheepfold of Christ. This is not exclusive of those who originally were prepared from the beginning as they were always of the sheepfold of Christ but a prepared people are those who have washed their garments who have agreed they are in need of the saviour's help (Rev 7:14) and GOD is not ashamed to be called their GOD. (Hebrews 11:16)

For whom he did foreknow, he also did predestine to be conformed to the image of his son, that he might be the first born among many brethren...whom he did predestinate, them he also called and whom he called them he also justified and whom he justified, them he also glorified(Romans 8:29-30).

Chapter 6: Wait Daily

Part of my early experiences with GOD included a fasted life, attending of vigils and regular attendance of fellowship and church services. And I will tell you this has greatly shaped my Christian life, That it has been easy to not allow your belly to be your GOD, A life of self control will earn you alot, especially when you can overcome anger in yourlife, I have been put on surveillance by the almighty in that respect.

When you can wake up and engage in quiet time, still kneel down at night and give GOD thanks for the day or take out an hour in your day to communicate with GOD you will find it easy to be that person GOD wants you to be. As a child I started with a club called Christian video network where we as children used to meet on either 2nd Saturdays of the month or 2nd to the last Saturdays of the month, and notwithstanding my naughty way of life,GOD still drew me to his son Jesus, I recall a dream I had as a child wherewith I was at the gate of heaven and I was told by my friend who was the security guard that I couldn't enter heaven and I heard a voice say Chinenye you have been a bad girl or a bad child I can't remember the exact words but I did fall from a high mountain or high statute wooden and fall into my body and jump up sideways, that was an early experience with GODs spirit. At secondary school I took services seriously, was a part of a fellowship called the Army, used to attend a program called Preview held by Mr Ademosun for we the girls of the protestant church community and eventually got baptised at the yaba Baptist church in 2004, when I was in ss1. Although I did Baptism by immersion again at the Lords Chosen Charismatic Revival Ministry. All this improved my waiting with GOD, and GOD being faithful kept drawing me to a life of devotion to him and a holy life.

Taking out time with GOD will earn you alot of sharpening by GODs spirit and it will prepare you not just for what is ahead but for his glory ahead.

You may need to wait daily to be able to plunge into that place GOD wants you to be or to be able to carry out the divine task he has for you, whether in marriage, or your profession, career, ministry or business, but if you can't gain GODs counsel at the time he expects you to, you may just never prepare for him or anything. Remember his words *if the bridegroom cometh will the bride be ready?* When I came to Lagos in 2016 because my marriage was not working, I applied to the local government chairman to get a spot to carry out legal work at the court premise, it did pay because that was a trying time and I was always provided for by GOD, then getting a job as a secretary every 3months because I deviated from GOD and wasn't paying close attention I did lose interest in the job, things became tight and I eventually resigned; stopped the job. Also working at a chamber, things turned ugly and within 3 months I lost the job, so I waited I ended up waiting by GOD from may till December and here I am able to do exactly what he wants from me, able to answer his call because I let him help me. Every time I applied for Jobs I resorted to him, one of the jobs I got was as an admin manager but I didn't pick up the job again for having that leading to still wait, it was annoying and felt wrong but it was for GOD to be able to reach me.

Beloved GOD can't talk to you if you are too busy with your dealings and not what he wants you doing. It doesn't mean you can't work or run that business but it means that you may just be wasting your time or not doing that one thing which he wants from you that will prepare you or launch you to bring about his desired end for your life. Why run away from waiting, is it the idea of a fast, Isaiah 58 stipulates on how to fast and Jesus said when he the bride groom is not around you would need to fast. This few months I waited, I did get divine visitations and I did get to remember things which I long for-got and this even made me marvel because I obeyed the leading of the holy spirit. See you must understand that many a time people around you may be used by your enemy to truncate the purpose of GOD for your life, they do it in ignorance because they are un-aware, they may even be used by GOD to test you, and GOD may hide it from them in order to mould you to the way he wants you to be. The devil may likewise use people to tempt you. If you go by GODs word you will be pre-pared by GOD and you won't miss out on GOD.

Chapter 7: Resist the Devil and He will flee from you

Resist the enemy, I didn't say wake up and keep saying die, die, die to your enemies, I said resist the enemy; you would need a lot more words than die, die, die. In ones work with GOD you will have to learn that taking a defense against Satan is more than binding and casting, it will include the fruits of GODs spirit and the application of the word of GOD, if you are lucky to be one who has the gift of speaking in tongue then it gives you a better edge, it did work for me in the year 2016. That period I was not in good health and the devil used to take advantage of me, I remember running away from the house for wanting to avoid his appearing despite the fact that GODs spirit was with me and I stayed at a motel at Eric Moore street Surulere, I couldn't afford a hotel room at that time, and one day I stayed in the room while there I knew he was interested in appearing, I resisted it, I could see him appearing already with his black wings but GOD being merciful he didn't again, I used a medium which I would expound on in the latter chapter of this book as GOD permits me and In my trying Christian times, I learnt to resist alot

Believers are to put on the breast plate of righteousness, the helmet of salvation, the belt of truth, the shoe with readiness to proclaim the gospel of peace and the sword of the spirit.The prepared people will be able resist the devil if they are adorned in this fashion. This is to enable them resist the devil and resist him in the entirety...

Chapter 8: Fight the good fight of Faith (A bit on thought Life)

Theres a fight of faith that every believer must engage in, it's only possible by our insistence on relying on the word of GOD, situation may want you to change your confession or mind set, but remember a double minded man cant receive from GOD. You are of one mind for being a born again, it is unbeliever that have double mind but a believer may succumb to that mind by letting those thoughts of lies projected by the enemy prevail or rule over you. One of the things I did learn in preparing as a person for

GOD was to change my thought pattern, I first made prayer points concerning my thoughts and it did work. Then I began to apply my prayer to my life, I likewise used the word of GOD to reinforce victory and I learnt to give reply at every voice I hear which most time was only interested in subverting the good plans GOD had for me. I would tell myself this is a lie and a deception of the devil, and sometimes I would insist I am in the arena of salvation and arena of covenant and I did quote a scripture and gain peace. I learnt that from a particular ministry I love even though am not down with some-things done there but I love the confession of one of the workers that insisted this is the arena of Liberty; it warmed my heart to hear that. So I had that hardness on my face insisting that I the ministry in which I attend is the arena of salvation and arena of covenant and it did remind me of the good that I required from GOD.

You would have to change your mindset and your confession to be able to stand out as a prepared people, you can't continue in that mediocre mentality because things did not go as planned or because those around you are unaware of your timing or the situation you are faced with or the trial you go through that for that reason you won't be qualified for the things of GOD or for the rapture. When I lost my Job in the chamber and after I watched some Christian programs on youtube all I got was testing and trying, infact prior to that time I was always having near accident experiences, crossing the road almost seemed impossible even taking a stroll to the market would appear that a car would want to swerve towards me or a motor-cycle hit me, I dreaded crossing the road, so going to church I cultivated the habit of using the overhead bridge in getting to the other side of the road. I like wise learnt to cross the road by demarcation and even use zebra crossing. I was attacked in my brain I remember visiting the doctor and complaining to him of bruxism and pains in my head that felt like nerve pains, he gave me some drugs and it did help but along the use of the drugs my lord Jesus asked me to put my hand on my head and receive healing and I got healing. While writing this book, I committed practically everything into GODs hands and the rest is between he and I, that's why it's possible because I did almost forget things I want to write and I usually asked the spirit to remind me and he being faithful he reminds me. The devil never stopped in disturbing my thought life, he used to engage me in dialogue most of which was to find fault with me or make me angry and he found out that I don't have anger he did it sometimes telling me things about my family to make me annoyed, most of the things that have transpired in my life regarding my thought life I don't recall but one thing I did say is that Jesus has been faithful. Being told to commit suicide and I refused by an image I don't

know and so much with the devil always trying to frighten me or do something against me,
somehow all that has transpired seemed to fade
away, during those times I recall pleading Jesus
always and telling the Satan that I can't reject
Jesus. Honestly people so much have happened
but you and me can win against Satan by staying with Jesus and keeping his commandments
doing what Gods spirit says we should.

The fight of faith must not stop, A people of GOD
can be prepared if they are high in faith, they
can live by faith, grow by faith and walk in faith.
Remember Hebrews 12, the forerunners of faith
obtained GODs promises by believing. If GOD
says to you that he has done something for you

or would do something, you are to believe and

walk in that revelation. That is the expectation

of GOD for you.

Chapter 9: Quench the fiery darts of the enemy

This the enemy that lures men into resisting the will of GOD and refusing GODs spirit to rule and reign. You will be able to quench the fiery darts of the enemy when you realise that the weapons of your warfare are not physical but carnal to the pulling down of strongholds that you wrestle not against flesh and blood but against all principalities.

When I took a particular important decision which greatly paid, the outcome is the books that GOD has enabled me to write, I got disturbed when writing by a particular Spirit in Black and some others too. But GOD was faithful protecting me and knowing my frame and even preventing me from seeing those spirits most times. I would always remind myself that this is the work I must do for GOD and that it's not about me but that I must write what he wants me to write.

Now that you can resist the devil and he flee from you, that you can fight the good fights of faith quenching the fiery darts means that you have to change your life in line with your victory, If you were a prostitute before and have stopped prostitution, don't wear those jewelleries again, don't where those garments again infact burn all those clothes and get new garments that are modest,change your outlook,if you were a lesbian before and you dressed like a man before,now that you are freed from lesbianism, you would need to tell that lesbian spirit that you are no longer interested by changing your garments, no more guys wears,you buy new skirts and new shirts and new sandals or shoes that make you look feminine, you even go to the extent of staying away from your lesbian partner and praying GOD for a marriage partner.

If you are a married man and you had a female friend who you were interested in marriage and she declined and now you are married, you may need to end whatever friendship you had with that woman or you invite your wife into that

friendship because the devil is very cunning

subtle and may be interested in using any me-

dium to plunge a fiery that at you, thereon be

wise as serpents and gentle as doves, Jesus said

we should pray that we don't enter into temp-

tation. The prepared people of GOD have learnt

to expose the cunning craftiness of the devil,

they are not naive,they are no longer deceived,

they are aware of the position of things and they

insist that they have identified with Jesus and

will rather stay with him. If you can't quench

the fiery dart*s of the enemy, how can you resist*

the devil and he flee from you they either go

hand in hand or are used interchangeably, Is the

devil your Father or is Jehovah GOD your father.

Choose this day whom you will serve.

74

Chapter 10: The Overcomer

I am in the arena of Salvation and the arena of covenant,I am not confused as to the state of my calling,I am free and free indeed,I am identified with Christ and I am qualified by his mercy and grace to be a heir of his kingdom.

I cant change my mindset, I have come too far, **for its written... lest any man take your crown.**

When anything happens all you say is that this is the device of the devil deception, to cause me to derail to destroy my faith, to kill my Joy, to take heaven away from me and then say no to the devil.

My body is the temple of the holy spirit, GODs gifts are going to make room for me, the fruits of the spirit give me peace and make me better in my relationship with people, Now I can say I have overcome by the blood of the lamb and the word of my testimony, My righteousness is like a filthy rag, but if I rely on the right-eousness of Christ through his word, I will pre-vail, He would not be ashamed to be called my GOD. I am an over comer. I will not be dis-graced because the sovereign GOD helps me. The over comer is prepared for GODs king-dom; he has overcome by the blood of the lamb and the words of the testimony of Jesus. That is the way to overcome the evil one.

Heaven is a glorious abode prepared by GOD for his children, GOD prepares his people daily and is interested that you and me get there or are able to return home. Let the mind of Christ be in you. Christ says be perfect as your heavenly father is. GOD will help us we can do this we a GODs people, his own prepared people.

A runner taking part in the Olympics to represent his country undergoes enough training and observes his do's and don'ts list for the period before his game. Hence with GOD we are representatives and GOD gives us do's and don't and expects us to readily prepare ourselves for him. Be an overcomer.

Chapter 11: Heavenly Mindedness

To be spiritually minded is life eternal, but to be carnally minded is death.

Now that you are an overcomer, as a pre-pared people you are minded about the things of GOD, you bare the mind of Christ, you carry the heavenly consciousness,you are happy going to church, the brethren make you happy, passing by the church lights up Joy within you, You are a carrier of the presence of GOD, you are unashamed of anything your past does not destroy you but define you. The

word of GOD lives in your heart and you carry
it everywhere with you. You refuse to be deceived.

You look forward to being a part of GODs kingdom, you look forward to the rapture,you envisage the glory of GODs kingdom and then you just think what will be the way of life in GODs kingdom. You have visions of heaven, dreams of his glory ahead and you are glad to be a born again.

You value your salvation and you are unwilling to lose it at every expense.

Matt 6:33 says seek the kingdom of GOD first and his righteousness and every other thing shall be added unto you.

When you have overcome your eyes are set on Christ. You are overwhelmed with the love of GOD and his joy fills your heart. All around you is Jesus you see. You are minded about the kingdom of GOD, the church and you only want to be with Jesus.

Jesus told Martha that Mary has chosen a better way. You can choose that better way by coming into the sheep fold and being amongst GODs own people. Be minded about GOD, he will prepare us for his kingdom. Amen.

Chapter 12: Now I can say I am prepared and "He" prepares me still

Hallelujah!

Now I can say I am prepared, for the glory ahead and he prepares me still, why? Because now we are the sons of GOD and it does not appear what we shall be..., We are know in part and later we shall come to know in full.

So Praise the lord!

Hosanna in the Highest.

The prepared people are the sons of GOD and they are still being prepared by GOD for greater things to come, they are beloved by GOD and they shall not be dismayed. They will walk in robes so white and wear the crowns prepared for them, they will eat from the tree of life because they sought a country not made with human hands whose architect and maker is GOD. They are GODs own people *– A chosen generation, a royal priesthood, a peculiar people, A holy nation, call forth to show forth the praises of him that called you out of darkness to his marvellous light. Ist Peter 2:9, Blessed and Holy is he that hath part in the first resurrection, on such the second death hath no power, but they shall be priests of GOD* *and of Christ, and shall reign with him a thousand years. Revelation 20 verse 6.*

Chapter 13: The Believer/ The Born Again

Are you a believer praise GOD, are you born again, thank your wonderful saviour! Are you allowing GOD prepares you for that glorious kingdom?

"For GOD so loved the world that he gave his only begotten son that whosoever believe in him will not perish but have everlasting life, John 3:16. Our GOD is wonderful; he is glorious preparing thousands of people every one in him he prepares still. You and me are not left out. His doing a great work willing that we live eter-

nally with him in heaven and that new heaven and new earth we are certainly not left out of it.

You too can win souls to Christ, talk to your neighbours, friends, family, tell GOD to help you. Brighten up on life because you are a believer and you should not perish but have everlasting life. Hallelujah! Amen.

Welcome to GODs Kingdom people!

Chapter 14: The demanding a sign

The bible says an evil and adulterous generation demand a sign but no sign will be given them but the sign of Jonah repent for the kingdom of GOD is at hand.

Instead this is a call to us to truly repent. GOD's kingdom   has come to stay, no need to resist his will, no need to reject GODs kingdom. Let the love of Christ truly flood your hearts and fill it. Don't be unbelieving seeking a sign when all before its glaring that Jesus is lord. I tell you no letter of the law has passed away until it is fulfilled. Now we have grace we too can be saved by

Grace.

The grace of GOD has been revealed to many and

has come to us all. I say choose life that you may

live. Amen

Hallelujah!

Chapter 15: Some statements of Jesus to some people in encounters that he had with them

I have permission from Holy Ghost to use from this write-ups but I think that there are salient statements made by Jesus with certain people who have had encounters with him which I believe I should share with the public. My Apology to whomsoever this may offend.

Here are some:

Mary Baxter: Jesus words to Mary Baxter, tell

the people that hell is real, that men and

women must repent of their sins.

Jesus says of a man in hell:

You not only distorted and misrepresented

the Holy word of GOD, but you lied about your

not knowing the truth. The pleasures of life

were more important to you than the truth.

Angelica Zambrano:

Daughter he is in this place (talking about hell)

because anyone who rejects my word already

has a judge.

Yes Daughter, but it is necessary to forgive be-

cause they have not forgiven many people and

that is why many people are in this place because they failed to forgive (still speaking of

hell)

Choo Thomas:

Jesus Words "It does not matter how good

people are, whoever doesn't know me, this is

the only place he will go(still speaking of hell)

Valley of the Shadow of Death:

He took me to another high mountain from

which I could look down into another endless

valley where a multitude of people dressed in

gray-colored robes were wandering about in

an apparent mood of dejection.

Their robes reminded me of the gowns worn

by hospital patients.

The people looked weak and lost, and their gray faces matched the color of the robes they were wearing. They stared at the ground in front of their feet as they walked around in circles, aimlessly and hopelessly. This place was mostly men with just a few women.

"Who are these people, Lord?"

"They are the sinful 'Christians.'"

"What is going to happen to them?" I wondered aloud.

"Most of them will go to the lake of fire after the judgment."

I wondered why these people were here, and

then I remembered

that their valley leads to the burning pit.

These so-called "Christians"

who don't really know the Lord and who con-

tinually and willfully sin

and don't repent before they die or before the

Rapture happens will

be eternally lost.

Romans 1:29-32, Galatians 5:19-21, and

Revelations 21:8 all are examples of how

some Christians live. Someone once asked

me how sinful Christians could enter Heaven.

We all must appear before the judgment seat

of Christ to receive what is due to us for the

things done while on earth, whether good or

bad. see 2 Corinthians 5:10.

"My daughter, this is why I keep telling you about the importance of Obedience and purity," Jesus said.

And if you are left behind, no matter what it cost don't ever, ever take the mark of the beast 666.

Rebecca Brown:

He 'GOD' says to MD Rebecca Brown, "Don't make the mistake of thinking that I have the same weak emotions as you humans have. I have no weaknesses and neither do I have the emotions you humans are so fond of attributing to me. You need to take heed of my words in Isaiah. Isaiah 55:8,9.

You hesitate to share my word because of your fear of offending someone. I tell you in truth, it will not matter to me how many tears are shed or how much anguished pleading for mercy occurs, and not one single person shall enter heaven except through my son Jesus!

Pg 66, Prepare for War by Rebecca Brown MD.

Joel 3:14:

"Multitudes multitudes in the valley of decision for the day of the lord is near in the valley of decision"

CHOOSE THIS DAY WHOM YOU WILL SERVE; CHOOSE LIFE AND YOU WILL LIVE

Conclusion

Is there a better way to salvation than the one that Christ has released unto us. A prepared people will be with GOD in eternity.

Salvation cry is heard in the street. Man must answer the call for life. You can't afford to be among the lost. GOD is coming for a spotless church.

Appreciation

I return thanks to GOD who has made this possible, who was a wall of fire around me. Thanks to my parents who GOD used in their own way to care for me, Chinwendu my sister who rendered help to me at odd times, The Lords chosen Ministry used by GOD to greatly help me. Pastor Whoaba who was of spiritual and financial assistance to me, MD Hoff deco who GOD used to render me financial assistance at the least of all times to receive even though in expectation and my Chuks who was an instrument in GODs hand in plunging me into this great ministry.

It wouldn't have been Possible without you

Lord Jesus Christ, the fairest of ten thousand

to my soul.